EGMONT

We bring stories to life

First published in Great Britain 2002 by Egmont Books UK Ltd
This edition first published in 2021
2 Minster Court, London EC3R 7BB
www.egmontbooks.co.uk
Text copyright © Julia Donaldson 2002
Illustrations copyright © Lucy Richards 2002
The moral rights of Julia Donaldson and Lucy Richards have been asserted.

ISBN 978 0 7555 0140 3
34600/002
Printed in Italy by L.E.G.O. S.p.A.

A CIP catalogue record for this title is available from the British Library.

Egmont takes its responsibility to the planet and its inhabitants very seriously.
We aim to use papers from well-managed forests run by responsible suppliers.

For Gareth with love. LR

For everyone at Kirkcowan Primary School. JD

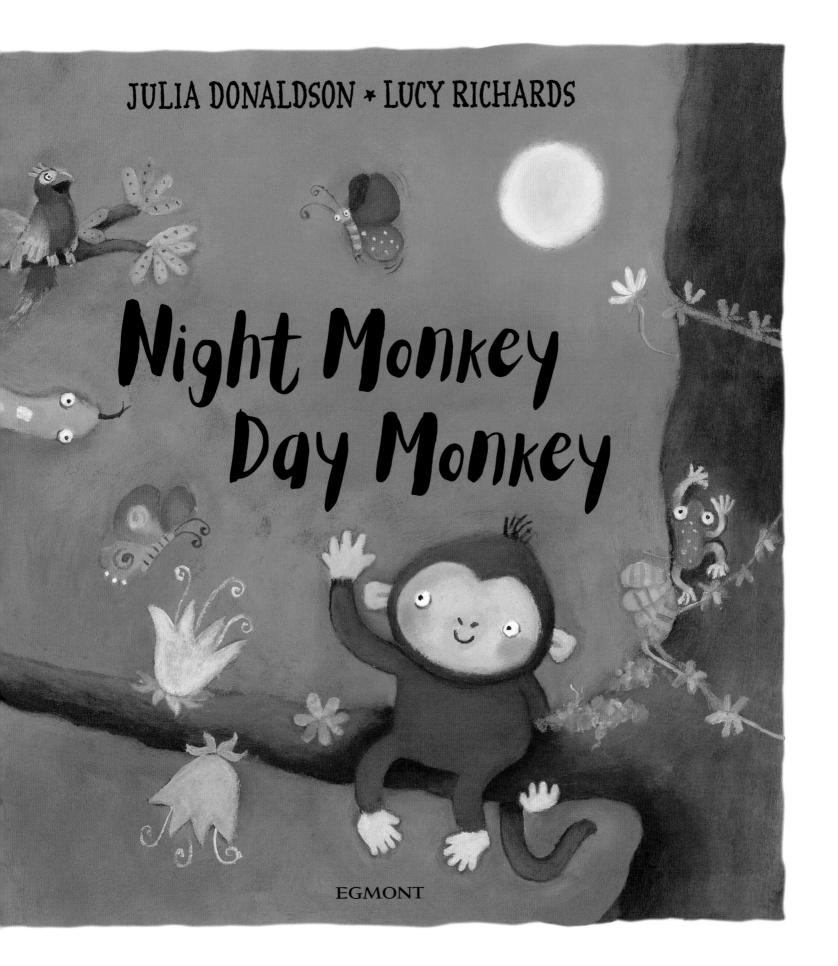

JULIA DONALDSON ★ LUCY RICHARDS

Night Monkey
Day Monkey

EGMONT

The moon shone down on the jungle.
Night Monkey climbed up the tree.
She clambered and leapt to where Day Monkey slept,
And whispered, "You can't catch me."

Day Monkey woke up and chased her,
But lost his grip on the bark.
He landed, cross, on a bed of moss,
Complaining, "It's much too dark!"

"Look!" said Day Monkey. "Hundreds of eyes,
Winking and blinking and bright."

Night Monkey laughed and said, "Don't be daft,
They're fireflies that flash in the night."

"**Help!**" said Day Monkey. "Flying mice!
Or maybe I'm wrong and they're rats."

Night Monkey laughed and said, "Don't be daft,
Haven't you heard of bats?"

"Stop!" said Day Monkey. "Listen to that! They're sawing the tree into logs."

Night Monkey laughed and said, "Don't be daft,
It's only a chorus of frogs."

"**Hey!**" said Day Monkey. "There's a banana!
How does it manage to fly?"

Night Monkey laughed and said, "Don't be daft,
That banana's the moon in the sky."

Day Monkey yawned and rubbed his eyes.
"Maybe I'm dreaming," he said.
"Night-time is creepy and I'm feeling sleepy.
I'm going back to bed."

The sun shone down the next morning.
Day Monkey slid down the tree.
He slithered and leapt to where Night Monkey slept
And whispered, "You can't catch me!"

Night Monkey woke up and chased him,
Screwing her eyes up tight.
She came to rest in an empty nest,
Complaining, "It's much too bright!"

"Look!" said Night Monkey. "Moths wearing make-up!
Why are they in disguise?"

Day Monkey laughed and said, "Don't be daft,
They're beautiful butterflies."

"Help!" said Night Monkey. "Look at those giants
Swinging about in the trees."

Day Monkey laughed and said, "Don't be daft,
Those giants are chimpanzees."

"**Stop!**" said Night Monkey. "Screeching owls,
The colour of peas and carrots!"

Day Monkey laughed and said, "Don't be daft,
Haven't you heard of parrots?"

"Hey!" said Night Monkey. "Two naughty monkeys! Can't they keep out of our way?"

Day Monkey laughed and said, "Don't be daft,
Our shadows are here to stay."

Night Monkey yawned and rubbed her eyes.
"Maybe I'm dreaming," she said.
"Daytime is crazy and I'm feeling lazy.
I'm going back to bed."

Now Night Monkey sleeps in the daylight
And Day Monkey sleeps in the night,
But now and again at sunrise
When it isn't quite dark or light,

They share a bunch of bananas
Halfway up a tree.
Day Monkey calls it breakfast.
Night Monkey calls it tea.